CUENTO
DE LUZ

For Pem Tandin, who graced my life
and placed Bhutan in my heart.

- Virginia Kroll -

To Marc, my true love,
with whom I share the path of happiness.

- Nívola Uyá -

Snowbounds Secrets

Text © Virginia Kroll
Illustrations © Nívola Uyá
This edition © 2013 Cuento de Luz SL
Calle Claveles 10 | Urb Monteclaro | Pozuelo de Alarcón | 28223 | Madrid | Spain
www.cuentodeluz.com

ISBN: 978-84-15784-72-2

Printed by Shanghai Chenxi Printing Co., Ltd. September 2013, print number 1395-4

FSC
www.fsc.org
MIX
Paper from
responsible sources
FSC® C007923

Snowbound Secrets

Virginia Kroll & Nívola Uyá

"Please, Papa, let me go, too," begged Pem. "I'm a good yak-herder."

"Yes," Papa agreed. "But now the snow is deep in places. Go to sleep and dream of summer."

"Papa, please!" Pem tried again.

"If you keep whining, Yeti will get you," warned Pem's big brother, Bhim, grabbing her and growling.

"Oh, Bhim," squealed Pem, squirming away. "You're just trying to scare me." Still she wondered. Did hairy mountain monsters really capture troublesome children?

At dawn, Pem was wide awake and winter-dressed as Bhim and Papa piled packs on the herd. "Pleeease," Pem asked once more.

Mama wrapped Pem's warmest woolen shawl around her small, sturdy shoulders. "You may go, Daughter," she said. When it came to decisions involving the children, a mother's word was law. Pem hugged Mama tightly, then hurried to join Papa and Bhim for her first-ever mountain journey.

Pem liked how the crispness of new air filled her lungs and made her feel clean from the inside out. She imitated squeaks of teeny pikas skittering to their hide-and-seek spots. She liked the clap of the yaks' hooves as they hopped on rocks and clomped up hills. She watched the swishing of their shaggy flank fringe. Their soft snorts and grunts comforted her, and when she heard the cry of the sacred black-necked crane, she knew that all would be well along their trail.

Of all the yaks, Pem's favorite was cream-colored Karpo, whose name meant "fair one." She had been born last year to Nado, the dark one. Now she and Pem would learn the secrets of trail-trekking together.

Two windless days passed. The yaks plodded single-file on along pebbled paths, each stepping in the footprints of the hooves ahead, stopping to nibble moss and grasses, herbs and lichens wherever they grew.

When Pem's legs tired, Papa hoisted her atop Nado's strong back. "I love this whole wide world!" she shouted, gasping in awe at the scenery around her.

On the third day, right before nightfall, a blizzard blew in. Icy sleet like freezing needles pierced the skin on Pem's wind-burned face. The thick-coated yaks turned away from the wind and stood still. But young Karpo was confused and afraid. She skittered and jerked when Pem snatched her lead rope. Pem spoke soothingly, "Easy, Karpo, turn."

Karpo slipped. Pem grabbed her tufted tail to steady her… too late! Down the rocks they skidded, then slid. "Pem!" Papa's panicked voice wailed, but it and Pem's screams were gobbled by blowing snow.

Down Pem and Karpo spiraled, into a sea of swirling white. Pem's breath was whooshed away. She closed her eyes tightly. Then BUMP! into a bank of fluff she landed.

"Karpo, where are you?" she sobbed, and tears froze on her face. In the pitch-black night, only the snow shed a pale glow around her. Pem knew that Papa and Bhim couldn't reach her in the storm. She knew that she'd be alone till morning, and she had to find Karpo so that they could be alone together.

Pem heard a grunt. On her belly, she inched blindly toward the sound, slowly, to keep from tumbling off another rocky ledge. "Karpo," she called, trying to sound brave.

Pem's whole body ached. Suddenly she felt a furry foot. "Karpo!" she yelped, gripping the hairy coat and pulling herself up by its thickness. But this was not the feel of Karpo's fur!

Pem looked up. Eyes glimmered, peering into hers. Not Karpo's round, brown, long-lashed eyes, but the squinty eyes of something… someone. Yeti! Pem fainted in terror.

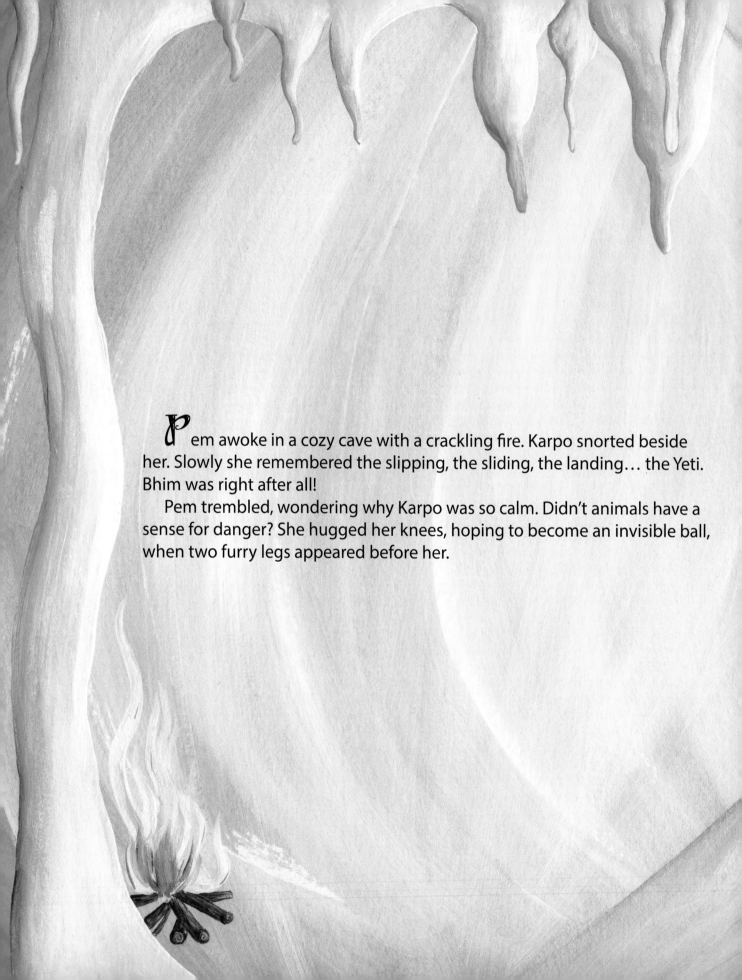

Pem awoke in a cozy cave with a crackling fire. Karpo snorted beside her. Slowly she remembered the slipping, the sliding, the landing… the Yeti. Bhim was right after all!

Pem trembled, wondering why Karpo was so calm. Didn't animals have a sense for danger? She hugged her knees, hoping to become an invisible ball, when two furry legs appeared before her.

Pem gazed upward and met the creature's face. She knew he was telling her, "Don't be afraid," though no words actually came from his mouth. He explained that she and Karpo were bruised, but otherwise fine. Somehow he knew she felt hungry and held out a handful of nuts and grains. His thoughts came from his brain, through his eyes, and right into Pem's. Back and forth they transferred questions, answers, and feelings while Karpo chewed the mound of hay that Yeti had provided.

Pem told Yeti about how grown-ups frightened children with tales about his kind. Yeti told Pem about hunters and why he must stay hidden. Pem told Yeti about home. Yeti understood all about family and asked if he could trust her. Pem promised him that he could.

Yeti made sounds like words that Pem couldn't understand. From the shadows, a female Yeti appeared with twins about Pem's size. They all stared, one as curious as the next.

The twins pulled Pem to a wall deep within the cave. In the firelight, she saw drawings of familiar animals with black-necked cranes flying above them. There were drawings of the twins and their parents and one of a human with a gun. This cave wall, Pem realized, told the story of this family's life.

One of the twins handed Pem a pointed stone, and the other patted the wall. Pem understood. She added a sketch of herself and Karpo, and they thanked her with smiles. Now Pem was part of their story, too.

When tiredness overtook her, she lay down between the twins. Just before she fell asleep, Yeti eye-promised Pem that he would lead her and Karpo back to Papa and Bhim tomorrow. Pem blessed Yeti with a promise of her own.

As dawn greeted a calm new day and the sun's rays dappled the entrance to the cave, Yeti told Pem that it was time to go. Pem, the twins, and their mother stared goodbyes into each other's eyes. Then Yeti led Karpo out and hefted Pem onto her back.

They traveled the trail in silence until a black-necked crane cried, and Pem heard Bhim and Papa calling her name. Pem and Yeti exchanged one last look, then he vanished.

"I'm here, Papa," Pem yelled over and over. When Papa came into view, Karpo's footsteps quickened. Pem leaped from her back into Papa's arms, and they tumbled to the ground in a tangle of joyful hugs.

At breakfast, Pem stroked Karpo's leg and talked about how scared she'd been. Bhim said, "Good thing Yeti didn't get you."

Pem smiled. "It was a good thing," she said, keeping her promise to Yeti and hugging the secrets with all her heart.

China

Nepal

Yeti's cave

Pem's house

Bhutan

India

Author's note

This tale takes place in Bhutan, a country in southern central Asia that is bordered by India, China, and Nepal. It is isolated from much of the world by mountains, ice, and snow. Ninety percent of Bhutanese people are farmers, and many of them herd yaks, hearty, powerful beasts of burden that are related to oxen.

Yaks carry heavy loads, including mail, through winding, rugged mountain pathways. They also provide milk, butter, cheese, and wool. Meat and skin are used after a yak dies, and when wood is unavailable, yaks' dung is burned for fuel. Yaks mate in September or October, and nine months later, the female delivers a single calf, which nurses on her nourishing milk for an entire year.

Summer in the Himalayas brings blooms, such as azaleas, rhododendrons, and the Himalaya blue poppy, whose petals feel like paper. Black-necked cranes, which can live for eighty years, are sacred because they are thought to be reincarnated beings that have come back to help people gain spiritual wisdom. Of the animals that the twins drew on the wall, such as takins, tigers, snow leopards, pygmy hogs, black bears, and red pandas, some are endangered species.

Weather can be harsh in the Himalayas, especially as winter approaches. If a storm arises, yaks usually turn their faces from the wind and wait it out calmly and comfortably. They have thick, woolen undercoats that keep them warm and shaggy overcoats that hang down around their legs. Wild yaks are dark brown, but domesticated yaks like the ones Pem's family herds come in a variety of colors.

The people of Bhutan believe that three types of big-footed creatures, called yetis or migois (strong men), live in the Himalayas. The large, man-sized ones, like the yeti whom Pem encounters, have cone-shaped heads and are known to be very kind.

There are several accounts of lost or injured travelers who claim to have been helped by yetis, who communicate not by speaking, but by thought-transfer, or mental telepathy.

Some have backward-facing feet, which may throw off the many hunters who try to track acapture them. In other areas of the world, Yeti is known as Bigfoot, Sasquatch, and Abominable Snowman. So widely accepted is their belief in the existence of yetis that the Bhutanese people have five postage stamps honoring them and the only yeti sanctuary in the world.

A few years ago, an educator from Bhutan asked me to write a story about her country so that children in other places could appreciate its beauty and uniqueness.

This is that story.